Slime Lake

Tom B Stone

Hodder
Children's
Books

a division of Hodder Headline plc

CHAPTER 1

His eyes were hurricane gray but darker. His beard looked like seaweed and tangled fishing nets. He wasn't smiling.

"He doesn't want us here," Marc Foster said to his twin sister, Terri. "Are you sure he's our uncle?"

"Your mother's uncle, your great-uncle," the twins' father reminded him.

"Of course he wants us here," said their mother. She leaned out of the car window and waved. Uncle Nicholas didn't wave back. He didn't smile. "You know he's always been like that."

"Yeah, but we've never had to spend the whole summer with him by ourselves before," muttered Marc.

Nicholas Lochmon, who'd been standing by the

wooden gate at the end of his dirt driveway when they arrived, swung it open and motioned them through.

"Uncle Nicholas! Hi! It's us," Terri called through her window.

"Duh," muttered Marc.

Terri was smiling at her uncle as her father cautiously eased the family's new car through the old gate. "I wonder how he knew when we'd get here? I guess he must have heard the car. And the road to his house is the only one at this end of the lake, isn't it, Dad?" Terri asked.

"If you call that a road," their father answered, clenching the steering wheel and trying in vain to steer the car between the ruts in the dirt driveway. He swerved suddenly to miss a big hole. A loud scraping sound came from beneath the car. "That's it!" Mr. Foster announced, turning off the engine. "The car stops here before we do permanent damage."

"You mean we're gonna have to carry our stuff the rest of the way?" Marc asked, outraged.

"It's not that far," said Terri cheerfully, bouncing out of the car. "Do you think it broke the car, Dad? What if you get stuck here and miss your plane?"

Marc turned to stare after her in disbelief.

It had to be true. Terri wasn't really his sister. They had been switched at birth. That was the only explanation for how completely different they were.

Like Terri's nonstop curiosity. She lived to ask questions. And if her hazel-green eyes were a little too intense while she waited for the answers, most people didn't notice it because her smile was so friendly.

Marc's smile was not friendly. He was good at leering, sneering, and jeering. But not basic smiling. And also unlike his twin, he was quiet and careful and deeply *not* into school.

And while Terri acted like their outgoing mother, Marc resembled neither their mother nor their work-until-you-drop father. If he and his sister hadn't looked so exactly alike, with their short black hair, brown skin, and hazel eyes, he might almost have believed that he wasn't really part of the family.

"Let's have some help here," said Mr. Foster, interrupting Marc's thoughts. Marc reluctantly got out of the car. A minute later he was staggering up the driveway to his uncle's house at the far end of Slime Lake.

The house was ancient, fifty times older than Uncle Nicholas even. The walls of big, weathered chunks of stone made the house seem to fade into the surrounding trees. A gently pitched slate roof punctuated by chimneys overhung the second storey. Attached to one end of the house was a round stone tower, which also had a slate roof.

Uncle Nicholas spent most of his time in the tower, or at least he did when they came up every summer to visit. Neither Marc nor Terri nor their parents had ever been inside it.

Why does he invite us if he doesn't even like us? Marc wondered for about the hundredth time.

And this year Uncle Nicholas had said Marc and Terri could stay for practically the whole summer while their parents went on a vacation of their own.

"Where are we going to sleep?" Terri asked, grinning over her shoulder at their uncle.

"Same as every year," said Uncle Nicholas, striding up behind them.

Terri giggled. "You tell us every year we can have any room in the house except yours."

"Same as every year," repeated Uncle Nicholas. He kept walking past them and up the broad, shallow stone steps into the house. By the time they'd followed him inside, he had disappeared into the kitchen with the bags of groceries Mrs. Foster had brought, as she did every year.

Mrs. Foster shook her head, smiling. "Okay, you two. You're on your own. Be good, now."

"Do what your uncle tells you," said their father, looking at his watch.

"Yes. He knows where to reach us in case of an emergency, of course. And don't forget to write," Mrs. Foster added.

"Yeah, yeah, yeah," said Marc, rolling his eyes.

4

"We'll miss you," said Terri.

Mrs. Foster laughed. "We'll miss you guys. But I know you two. Five minutes after you dive into Slime Lake, you'll have forgotten all about us!"

Marc looked over toward the kitchen doorway at his frowning uncle. "Don't be so sure . . . ," he mumbled under his breath.

Upstairs, Marc took the same room he always took, next door to his sister's and overlooking the lake. He opened a dresser drawer, unzipped his duffel bag, and held it upside down above the drawer.

"There," he muttered. "I'm unpacked." A minute later he was in the cutoffs he wore for swimming and for everything else in the summer. He pulled on a pair of grunged-out sneakers.

"I'm going down to the dock," he announced in a loud voice as he passed his sister's door.

"Wait for me! I'm almost ready!" he heard her cry. He smiled with satisfaction and took the stairs two at a time. He pushed open the heavy front door and walked quickly along the short path Uncle Nicholas kept hacked between the brambles. A moment later he stepped off the path and onto the worn planks of the old dock.

The flat-bottom rowboat wallowed in the water by the ladder at the dock's end as if it hadn't moved since they'd last tied it there the summer before. But Marc could tell that it had gotten a new coat of paint since then, and the life jackets in it looked new, too. Uncle Nicholas always took good care of things.

The water of the lake was green. Flat, opaque, almost milky green. Slime green. Even on a hot day like this one, with the sun beating down and glaring off the water, you couldn't miss that ominous alligator green.

That was where the lake got its name.

"Slime Lake," said Terri's voice at his shoulder. "Isn't it beautiful?"

"No," said Marc.

"You don't think so?" Terri threw out her arms as if she wanted to hug the whole lake.

"It's just a lake, Terri. Good grief." For some reason, Terri's enthusiasm was getting on his nerves.

Terri dropped her arms to her side and stared at him. Like Marc, she was wearing cutoffs. She was also wearing a faded yellow bathing suit underneath the cutoffs and a pair of plastic shoes that looked as if they were made out of melted pink jelly beans.

"I thought you liked Slime Lake," she said.

"I do. I just don't *love* it, okay? And haven't you ever wondered why Uncle Nicholas always invites us to spend the summer here?"

"No," said Terri. "Why would I? He asks us because he's our uncle. And because he's always asked us."

Marc shrugged.

Turning back toward the lake, Terri shaded her eyes. Uncle Nicholas's house was the only one at the far end of the lake. It stood next to the water and on the edge of what Mr. and Mrs. Foster called a wetland and what Marc and Terri called a swamp.

At the other end of the lake was a recreation area locally known as the Wreck. Near it, cabins could be glimpsed through the trees. Not far beyond that the only stretch of paved road for miles around ran past the Lakeside General Store, which sold gas and stamps and groceries.

Pops ran the Wreck. No one knew what Pops's real name was. He'd just always been there, short and round and wearing an eye patch to go with the wrecked-ship motif of his concession stand. He claimed that the concession stand really was all that was left of an actual boat he'd found half buried in the mud at the marshy end of the lake years before. "Left behind by pirates," he said, "when this lake was connected to the ocean. Before it dwindled into a swamp."

No one believed him, any more than they believed his stories about the monsters lurking in Slime Lake . . . also left behind by the receding ocean.

The Wreck concession stand sat at the back of the recreation area, surrounded by picnic tables scattered in the shade. Past the picnic tables was a flat skirt of sandy grass and then a half-moon of gritty, rocky lake beach. A T-shaped dock poked out from the middle of the beach, dividing it into a swimming area on one side and a boat-docking area on the other. One arm of the dock ended in a diving platform.

Terri made a face. "Let's go swimming. I'm *roasting*." She ran her hand up the short hair on the nape of her neck. "Look how sweaty I am!"

"I'll take your word for it," Marc said.

Making another face at her brother, Terri dropped her towel and began to yank off her cutoffs. She had one leg in and one leg out when Marc saw his chance.

He leaned forward.

Terri's eyes widened. She tried to get her other leg free, but one of her shoes got tangled up somehow. She made a vain effort to hop out of Marc's reach.

But she couldn't do it.

"Gotcha!" shouted Marc, and pushed his sister into the lake.

Terri hit with an enormous splash. Green water foamed up around her.

She rose to the surface, sputtering. Her cutoffs and one pink shoe floated up beside her.

Marc doubled over with laughter.

"Gotcha!" he shouted again.

"You—You—You—" she stuttered. "You are going to get it, Marc Foster!" She swam toward the ladder. "Wait'll I get my hands on you. I'm going to bury you. I'm going to throw *you* into Slime Lake. In little pieces. I'm—"

She stopped with a jerk. Her eyes widened.

"Marc?" she said, her voice going up.

She suddenly spun around in the water, as if something beneath the surface had slammed into her.

"Marc!" she screamed. "Marc, help m—"

Terri leaped up in a spray of foam, thrashing her arms wildly. Then she disappeared beneath the green water.

CHAPTER
2

"Ha," said Marc. He leaned over the edge of the dock to look down into the water where his sister had disappeared. "Ha, ha, Terri. Very funny. You think I'm going to fall for that?"

A few bubbles rose to the surface.

"Okay, Terri. It didn't work. You can come up now," he said.

Another string of bubbles appeared. Then, slowly, slowly, Terri's other pink plastic shoe floated to the top of the water.

"Terri!" said Marc.

His sister didn't answer.

Marc leaned over and stared hard at the place where Terri had gone under. Nothing. No bubbles. The water had flattened out to dead calm. It was as if his sister had never been there at all.

"Terri?" said Marc.

His sister still didn't answer.

Marc spun to face the shore. Nothing there, either.

He turned back around and squinted out over the still, almost gelatinous-looking surface of the lake.

It was flat and smooth and unbroken.

"Terri!" said Marc, suddenly afraid. "The joke's over, okay? Come on up. . . . Terri, come on! This isn't funny anymore. Terri! . . . *Terri!*"

One pink shoe floated closer to the dock. Hardly knowing what he was doing, Marc grabbed the old fishing net that hung off one of the pilings and leaned forward.

The shoe was just out of reach.

He straightened up. "*Terriiiii!*" he called. His voice echoed across the lake.

Panicking, trying to stay calm, he leaned over again. Had she caught her foot on something? Had . . . had something gotten her?

But what? He'd never even seen a snake in the lake—or even a very big fish. He felt himself break out into a terrified sweat. He wiped his forehead.

"Terri," he gasped, straining with the net to try and snag her shoe.

Suddenly he was sailing through the air.

He landed in the lake with a splash.

The lake was as cold as it was green. The frigid water

knocked the breath out of him. He opened his mouth and swallowed some water. And slime.

Lakewater had never been his favorite flavor.

He thrashed his way to the surface.

His sister stood on the end of the dock. As he treaded water, glaring up at her, she clasped her hands in front of her. "Oooh, Marc. Are you all right?" she asked in a high, silly-girl voice.

"You, you, *total* slime-sucker!" Marc gasped.

"Gotcha," Terri said, reverting to her normal voice.

"I can't believe you did that!"

"You started it," she said. "I can't believe you didn't hear me swimming under the dock to the shore, or walking down the dock and coming up behind you."

"I hope something *does* get you," said Marc. "See if I help you out."

But he wasn't really angry anymore. He was getting used to the water. It was summer. School was over. The next school year was weeks and weeks away.

"Come on in," he said. "The water feels good."

"I know," she said. She leaped into the air and can-nonballed into the lake.

The moment she hit, Marc grabbed her leg and yanked her under.

Then he was off, swimming out across Slime Lake, with his sister right behind him.

* * *

"Your turn to row," Marc said. They were headed for the Wreck.

Terri, who'd been kneeling in the front of the boat trailing her hand in the water, lifted it up. Thick strands of green oozed from between her fingers.

"Green spaghetti," said Marc.

"There's tons of this," she said.

"Tell me something new," said Marc, lifting up one oar. Slime coated the end of it.

"But there's lots more than ever before," Terri said. She frowned. "Do you think it's pollution?"

Before Marc could answer, a roar filled the air. From out of nowhere it shot through the water toward them.

"It's a motorboat!" shouted Terri. "And it's headed straight for us!"

She jumped up and snatched the cap from her head and began to wave it. "Hey! Hey, look out!"

At the last possible moment, the motorboat veered and missed them. Their rowboat lurched violently in the churning green wake of the huge, gleaming white boat. Terri flailed her arms wildly and barely saved herself from going overboard.

Marc caught a glimpse of a white yachting cap and dark glasses behind the tinted windshield of the motorboat. The words "Emerald Shores Princess," written in blinding green script on the bow of the boat, flashed past his eyes.

14

"You big jerk!" he shouted. He turned to Terri. "You okay?"

Terri was staring after the boat, which had become a white dot on the horizon. "It's a motorboat," she repeated in a stunned voice. "But motorboats aren't allowed on Slime Lake!"

The huge white boat was tied to the end of the dock when they rowed up to the Wreck.

And that wasn't the only thing that was different about the dock. As Terri nosed the boat close to the ladder and Marc climbed up it with the rope to tie their rowboat to the dock, they saw rows of canoes and rowboats lined up along the shore. A big white sign nearby said BOATS FOR RENT in big green letters.

Marc tied the boat up. Terri climbed the stairs to join him.

Terri pointed. "Look!" she said in a strangled voice.

A huge, gaudy new sign had replaced the plain old wooden one with THE WRECK on it above the concession stand. This sign said WELCOME TO THE EMERALD SHORES RECREATION AREA! HAVE FUN! The words "Emerald Shores" were written in blinding green script.

Worse, the Wreck concession stand was completely gone. In its place was a neat, square building glistening with blinding green paint, a color never seen in nature, not even in Slime Lake. Music blared over a set of loudspeakers attached to each end of the concession stand. All the picnic tables had been painted green, too. The only thing that hadn't been painted green was the dock.

"Look," said Terri again. Marc looked. He saw that the swimming area had been enclosed with a line of bright green-and-white buoys. The lifeguard who sat in the lifeguard's chair on the shore wore dark, dark glasses. Her blindingly white cap was emblazoned with the words "Emerald Shores."

"I've been abducted by aliens," said Terri, almost to herself. "This is a parallel reality. It's, like, like, virtual reality. It's not really real."

Marc pinched his sister's arm.

"Oww!" she said. "What'dja do that for?"

"To show you it is real," he said. He started forward again. "Come on." He trotted toward the concession stand.

Jaws Bennett was standing by the snack window, his jaws moving methodically.

Some things never change, thought Marc. Aloud he said, "Hi, Jaws."

"Hi," echoed Terri.

Jaws was a kid from Grove Hill, the town nearest to Slime Lake. He went to school with Marc and Terri.

A large boy who liked to eat, Jaws frequently boasted that he would eat anything, even dead rats.

Jaws nodded hello. His jaws kept moving.

"So, what's going on around here?" asked Terri.

Jaws looked around. He chewed some more. He swallowed. "Dunno," he said.

"May I help you?" said a brisk voice. The words sounded more like an order than an offer.

The three of them turned to see an athletic-looking man with receding blond and gray hair, a slightly receding chin, and pale blue eyes. He was standing behind the counter of the concession stand.

Marc blurted out the first thing that came to mind. "Where's Pops?"

The man frowned. "Why?"

"Because he's a friend of ours," said Marc.

"Pops has retired," said the man. "My name is George Quayle. I run Emerald Shores now." He gave Marc a hard look.

"This isn't Emerald Shores, this is Slime Lake," Marc began hotly.

Terri suddenly smiled and stuck out her hand. "Hello, Mr. Quayle. Is that your boat out there?"

Transferring his attention from Marc to Terri, Mr. Quayle paused before answering, as if he suspected Terri of some kind of trick.

Terri's smile was big and friendly.

Geez, thought Marc in disgust. *Why does she have to be friends with everybody? Can't she see this guy is a creep?*

But Mr. Quayle was smiling now, too. "It sure is," he said.

"Motorboats aren't allowed on Slime Lake. Never. Ever," said Marc.

"Says who?" said Mr. Quayle, his smile disappearing.

"Did you do all the work, fixing everything up and painting it green?" Terri went on, still smiling.

Mr. Quayle's smile reappeared. "It's just the beginning," he boasted. "There's gonna be condos, there's gonna be time-shares, there's gonna be a very exclusive hotel. Why, when I'm through with Emerald Shores, you won't even recognize the place."

"Emerald Shores! It's called Slime Lake," Marc repeated.

"Son, I can call it whatever I want . . . or I will, just as soon as a few details are worked out." Mr. Quayle narrowed his pale blue eyes. "There's a bad element around here who doesn't understand progress. They keep talking about the environment. Fresh water, clean air. Phooey. Nothing smells as good as money, that's what I say."

He waved in the direction of the lake. "Gonna

dredge it. Gonna have speedboats and Jet Skis and entertainment. It'll be a big-time resort, and they can't stop me. They tried to scare me off. Scared a few of the workers off when I was fixing up this recreation area. Strange noises. A monster! Huh!"

"Monster? Did someone really see it?" asked Jaws, forgetting to chew for a moment.

Mr. Quayle smiled slyly. "Of course there are monsters. See?" He pointed to a counter at one side of the concession stand. The three kids saw T-shirts, mugs, key chains, and dozens of other items. Every item was green and white and imprinted with the words "Emerald Shores" in blinding green script. Underneath the logo was a goofy-looking green cartoon monster.

"That's Emmie," Mr. Quayle said proudly.

"Emmie?" said Jaws in a puzzled voice. "Who's Emmie?"

"She's the monster from Emerald Lake. Great marketing idea! Maybe I'll even set up monster hunts! Pay someone to dress up like a monster and rock the boat a little. You know, like Disney World or something."

A far-off look came into Mr. Quayle's eyes. "Why, Emmie could be just the beginning. This lake could be part of a huge theme park. . . . "

Marc and Terri and Jaws stared at the green figure on the front of the T-shirts. She looked a little like a brontosaurus but with the body of a seal. She had a big smile on her face and big, goofy eyelashes painted around her eyes.

"It looks like a warped Barney," Marc mumbled.

"But the monster in Slime Lake doesn't look like that," Terri added.

"There aren't any monsters!" said Mr. Quayle sharply. "It's a gimmick, see? Something to keep the tourists busy. To help them spend their money. That's what makes tourists happy, see? Keeping busy and spending money."

Mr. Quayle paused to take a breath.

"Do you mind if we look around?" asked Terri quickly.

Abruptly Mr. Quayle seemed to focus on Terri again. "Sure thing, little girl. Make yourself at home. Buy a T-shirt! Rent a canoe!"

"Not right now. But thanks, Mr. Quayle," said Terri politely.

"You can call me George," he said.

"I know what I'd like to call you," Marc said under his breath as they walked away.

"If you do, I'm gonna tell Mom and Dad," said Terri.

Marc rolled his eyes. They walked silently down to the swimming area.

"Look!" said Jaws. "A lifeguard!"

They stared at the lifeguard sitting motionless up in the chair. She wore dark green sunglasses. Her swimsuit was emerald green to match the lettering on her hat. A green whistle hung on a white cord around her neck.

"Hey! Hi!" cried Terri, waving her arms.

The lifeguard turned her head slightly. She didn't wave back.

Undeterred, Terri charged across the beach to the lifeguard's chair. A huge new sign was posted by the chair, with a long list of rules for swimmers.

"Hi!" called Terri again. "My name is Terri. And this is Marc and Jaws."

"I'm so excited," said the lifeguard sarcastically. She blew the whistle and pointed at a little boy. "Stay out of the deep water!" she barked.

"What's your name?"

"Tiffany!" snapped the lifeguard. "Tiffany Quayle."

"Wow! Is Mr. Quayle your fa—"

"He's my uncle. I'm busy here, so push off!"

But Terri didn't give up easily. "Where's Pops?" she asked.

Tiffany dropped the whistle and bent her head to stare down at the three kids. The way she did it made Marc feel like an insect.

"Retired," she answered at last.

"Retired, like, where?" Terri persisted.

"What's it to you?" Tiffany practically snarled. "Are you gonna swim, or aren't you? 'Cause if you are, you have to obey the rules. And if you're not, I don't want you hanging around."

"We've got to go," said Marc before his sister could answer. He practically dragged her away, with Jaws following.

"You're not going, are you?" Jaws whined. "You just got here! We could have some lunch!"

"Later," said Marc.

To his surprise, his twin let him lead the way back to the boat. He was practically running by the time he got to the ladder.

When he stopped, he turned and saw Terri waving cheerfully in the general direction of the concession stand.

"Come *on*," he almost shouted. He grabbed his sister's arm and practically dropped her into the boat.

The sound of music thumping over the loudspeakers above the concession stand followed them halfway across the lake.

Neither of them spoke. At last Marc handed the oars over to Terri.

"Are you nuts?" he asked her. "Why're you being so friendly to that guy? He's ruining the lake!"

Terri shrugged and began to row. Her eyes were as green as the lake's on a stormy day. Then she said, "Why did Pops leave?"

"Gee, I don't know," said Marc, rolling his eyes. "Maybe the monster ate him."

"If there was a monster, he wouldn't eat Pops," she said.

Marc folded his arms in disgust. "You want a monster? I'll give you a monster. Mr. Quayle is a monster—in case you hadn't noticed!"

CHAPTER
3

"Mr. Quayle," Uncle Nicholas said in his raspy voice. "So you met the big man."

"Yes," said Terri.

Marc waited for his great-uncle to say more. But of course Uncle Nicholas didn't. He just kept dishing up white strands of spaghetti.

Marc suddenly remembered the slime on the end of the oar and swallowed hard.

They were sitting at the big, round, scarred oak table in the dining room of Uncle Nicholas's house.

"He has a motorboat, Uncle Nicholas," said Terri. "Isn't there a rule or something about no motors on the lake?"

Uncle Nicholas frowned. He didn't answer.

Terri kept on talking, about Mr. Quayle, about the

Wreck, about Pops. "Mr. Quayle said Pops had retired."

Uncle Nicholas glared. "Retirement!" he spat. "Hah!"

Why is Uncle Nicholas so touchy about retirement? wondered Marc. *It's not like he has a job he's gotta retire from.*

But their uncle's ferociousness had silenced even Terri. They ate the rest of their dinner without talking.

Personally, Mark preferred it that way. Although he wasn't too thrilled with the way Uncle Nicholas kept staring, first at him and then at his sister.

Of course, she didn't even seem to notice.

The days on Slime Lake could be fun, thought Marc. *But with Uncle Nicholas, the nights are definitely going to be bummers!*

Marc woke with a start.

The sound he'd heard hadn't been human.

"Aaaaahhhh. Aahhhhhhhhhhhooooooooh." It came again, a long, low, wailing sob.

It made the hair on Marc's neck stand up.

He'd never heard a sound like it in all the summers he'd spent at Slime Lake. It wasn't an owl and it wasn't a loon. It wasn't the human-sounding scream of a rabbit caught by a predator.

"*Aahhhhhhhhh.*"

Marc sat up.

He stared at his open window. He decided it might be a good idea to close it.

Of course, whatever it was probably couldn't come through the screen in a window on the second storey.

Could it?

"*Ohhhhhhhaha . . .*"

In a flash he was across the room, slamming the window shut.

There.

Then he saw her. A tiny figure at the end of the dock, outlined by the light of the half-moon.

His sister.

Great, thought Marc. *Just great.* His sister was making that sound! She had gotten him again!

Well, now it's your turn, Terri, he thought.

He yanked on a dark T-shirt and his jeans and jammed his feet into his black high-tops. A moment later he was letting himself quietly out the back door.

He slid around the side of the house. He was surprised that there were no lights on. Didn't Uncle Nicholas hear the noise?

Staying low and moving as quietly as he could, Marc made his way to the trail that led down to the dock. He straightened up.

Yes. She was still there.

As Marc ducked back down, he heard the sound again.

It made him stop for a moment. It was such an awful sound. A low, horrible, mournful wailing. It vibrated in the dark air, echoing off the dark water. It sounded like something dying.

Or something that had come back from the grave.

How was his sister doing that? No doubt about it. He had a twisted sister.

Marc began to inch his way down the path, keeping his ears open for the sound of footsteps on the wooden boards of the dock. That would mean his sister was coming back. If she did, he'd have to put Plan B into effect—jumping up and shouting boo.

But that was so childish.

He liked his first plan better. He was going to sneak out onto the dock, just as she had that morning. He was going to creep up behind her and scare her out of her wits.

And maybe push her into the lake, just for good measure.

He'd reached the end of the dock. He put one foot on it, then the other. Slowly, carefully, he made his way, one plank at a time, toward his sister.

She never moved. She stood rigidly in her pale nightshirt, staring out across the dark water.

A breeze whispered in Marc's ear. He heard lapping against the dock. It was a hungry sound.

But, he told himself, it helped hide any noise he might make.

He crept closer.

Closer.

She remained motionless.

"Aha!" he cried. "Gotcha!"

He sprang forward.

Terri didn't move.

Marc stopped in midgrab. His hands dropped to his side.

"Terri? Are you trying to psych me out or something?" He walked around in front of his sister.

The breeze made her nightshirt eddy around her like a ghostly shroud. It was the only thing about her that didn't seem to be carved out of stone. She was staring straight ahead, sightlessly, out over the lake.

Marc raised his hand and waved it in front of his sister's eyes. She didn't even blink.

She was like a statue. Like one of those statues in the old graveyard on the hill above their school in Grove Hill.

Then the sound filled the dark air around them again.

But it wasn't Terri after all.

It wasn't Terri who was making the horrible hungry sound that was coming from beneath the dock right below their feet. . . .

CHAPTER

4

"Terri!" he shouted so loudly, that anybody would have been able to hear him at the other end of the lake. *"Terri, come on!"*

He grabbed his sister and spun her around.

Something slammed against the planks of the dock. The whole dock shook.

He jerked Terri's arm as hard as he could. She fell stiffly forward, then stumbled.

And stopped.

The thing howled again and hit the dock. It was like an earthquake. Marc almost lost his footing and fell into the lake.

This time it was Terri who saved him. She caught him by the sleeve of his shirt and pulled him back.

"Marc!" Terri's eyes were wide and dark. And terrified. "Marc, what's going on? How did I get here?"

"Later," said Marc. "First we have to get out of he—" The water around the dock seemed to boil into life.

Marc didn't wait to see what was about to rear its ugly head. He took Terri's arm and shot up the dock at top speed.

"Help! Help! *Monster!*" he shouted as he ran. A monstrous scream of rage followed them up the path. It seemed to yank at Marc's legs.

He kept running. As he ran the sound receded. Died to a whimper.

And then it was gone.

Marc dragged his sister through the front door of the house, slammed it, and locked it behind him.

"Huh, huh, huh," he heard himself panting, like a big dog.

He pulled Terri into the kitchen, and they both sat down at the kitchen table.

Suddenly the lights came on.

Marc jumped and screamed.

Uncle Nicholas stood at the back door of the kitchen, his eyes angry, his face twisted into a scowl.

"What is going on here?" he roared.

Terri looked at Marc. Marc looked at Terri. His sister still looked pretty out of it.

"Terri had a nightmare," said Marc. "About, ah, monsters. Yeah, that's it. Monsters."

Scowling, Uncle Nicholas stomped across the

kitchen. The twins shrank back as he brushed by.

"It's the middle of the night. Get some sleep!" he ordered. "Monsters," they heard him muttering as he walked out.

Marc stared down at the floor. He looked at his sister again. She had her head turned toward the door. Her expression was vague and dreamy, as if she were still asleep.

Terri hadn't noticed it, then. But Marc had. Uncle Nicholas had been wearing his boots under his bathrobe. And the boots had been covered with fresh green slime.

"Terri! Terri, it's me. Marc."

"I'm awake."

Marc pushed the door to his sister's room open and, with a quick glance down the hall in the direction of Uncle Nicholas's tower, slipped inside.

He hadn't been able to go back to sleep. He knew that his twin hadn't been able to, either.

Terri was sitting on a chair she'd pulled up to the window. Her room was dark. "Don't turn on the light," she said as Marc reached for the switch.

"What are you doing?" he asked.

"I'm not sure."

Marc went over to the window to stand beside her. "You heard it, didn't you?"

"I'm not sure," she answered slowly. "I think I did. But it was all confused with the dream I was having."

"What were you dreaming? Was it a nightmare? *Were* you dreaming about monsters?"

Terri shook her head. "No. It was just a voice. I mean, I don't remember anything except that I was talking to someone. Only it was in some other language."

"You don't know any other languages," Marc said impatiently. "I can't believe you didn't hear it! It was, like, moaning and howling. It's what woke me up. I thought it was you, playing a dumb joke, especially when I looked out the window and saw you standing on the dock."

Terri looked back out the window at the lake. The dock was a long dark finger, reaching out into the even darker water. The light of the half-moon made the weathered gray planks silver.

The dock looked solid and unshakable. The water was calm. Nothing gave any sign that something had battered against the pilings supporting the dock so hard that the dock had seemed about to collapse.

"I was sleepwalking," said Terri. "I don't know how I got out to the dock."

"Well, it's a good thing I came along when I did," said Marc. "Or the monster would have eaten you for sure."

"But I thought you didn't believe in monsters," said Terri.

"I do now," said Marc grimly. "I sure do now."

Marc was on monster alert the next day. And the next. And the one after that.

But nothing happened. The lake stayed calm. Terri slept through each and every night. Only owls and she-foxes and tree frogs called in the darkness, and the only disturbances in the lake were the occasional splashes of fish and of the people who had begun arriving for summer vacations.

At first Marc wouldn't go swimming at all. He watched his sister splash and dive and he sat on the end of the dock, keeping his eyes open.

"You're giving me the creeps," his sister complained. "You're like some wacked-out lifeguard or something."

Marc began to feel stupid. And hot. And water deprived. Finally he gave in.

The water felt fine.

"Race you out to the buoy," challenged Terri, pointing to the red-and-white buoy that floated near the center of the lake to mark the deep water.

"I can beat you swimming backwards," Marc answered instantly.

They splashed out toward the buoy. Just as Marc

was about to win, Terri grabbed Marc's foot and yanked him backward. She swam past him and slapped her hand against the buoy.

"I won!"

"You cheated!"

"I did not!"

"You grabbed my foot!"

"Did not!"

"Did too!"

"Did not!"

"Race you back." Marc pushed off and got a good head start.

"Hey! No fair!" Terri swam noisily after him.

I'm winning, thought Marc. Then Terri grabbed his foot.

Forget it, Terri, he thought, and kicked out. Her hand slipped off. He kept swimming.

She grabbed his foot again. Marc stopped and sputtered, "Hey!"

Then he saw Terri. She was still a long way behind him. And she wasn't even swimming.

"Terri," he called.

Terri looked past Marc. She raised one dripping hand. "Look out!" she screamed. *"Look ouuutt!"*

CHAPTER
5

It came toward him with a roar.

Marc froze.

"Go under!" he heard his sister shriek. "*Dive!*" Then she began to scream and wave her arms. "Look out! Look out! You're going to hit—"

Marc didn't hear the rest. He dove beneath the surface of the water as fast and as hard as he could. Down, down, down he plunged into the green depths. He thought his lungs would burst.

The huge motorboat passed over him, sucking and churning the water, as if it wanted to pull him back up into its shiny, evil propellers. It seemed to go on forever. Marc tried to swim out from under it. He could hear its enormous roar even deep beneath the surface.

His lungs were on fire. He couldn't stay under any longer. With a last, desperate pull and kick, to get himself as far away as he could from where he thought the boat was, he surfaced.

The boat had stopped only a few yards away.

It was huge. It was painted blinding white and had green trim. Somehow Marc was not surprised to see the name *Emerald Shores Princess* written in familiar green script on the side.

"Crazy kids!" he heard an angry voice shouting. "What are you doing swimming out here in the middle of the lake?"

"Because that's what the lake is for!" shouted Marc. "Swimming!"

"Marc! Oh, Marc, you're all right!" Terri swam over and stopped to tread water next to him. "You're not hurt?"

"No," said Marc. He raised his voice. "No thanks to you, Mr. Quayle!"

"You had no business being out here!" Mr. Quayle said. "Why don't you swim at the recreation area like you're supposed to!"

"We can swim anywhere we want to," said Marc. "You're not even supposed to have that boat on this lake."

"We're sorry if we frightened you, Mr. Quayle," said Terri suddenly.

"What?" said Marc. His mouth dropped open. He

swallowed what felt like half the lake and began to cough.

"What?" said Mr. Quayle. He leaned forward.

"Remember me? We visited you at the Wreck—the recreational center. Terri. We didn't mean to get in your way. We're just not used to seeing motorboats on the lake. We didn't even see you coming. It was like you came out of nowhere. . . . It's a beautiful boat."

Mr. Quayle, still suspicious, said, "Thank you."

"I bet it's fun to ride in," Terri went on.

"She's a regular rocket," said Mr. Quayle, patting the boat as if it were a living thing. Then he said, "I tell you what, just to show you there are no hard feelings, why don't I give you a ride to the Emerald Shores Recreation Center."

"You mean the Wreck?" asked Marc.

Both Terri and Mr. Quayle ignored him. "That'd be great," said Terri. "But we have to tell our uncle where we're going. And get money and towels and stuff." She pointed. "That's our dock."

Mr. Quayle looked over at the dock and at Uncle Nicholas's house. "So you're visiting old Nicholas Lochmon?" he said. Then he said, "Come on, climb aboard. I'll just nudge this baby up to the dock and you can get what you need to go to the recreation center."

A few minutes later Marc and Terri were sitting in

the huge boat, feeling the powerful surge of the motor as Mr. Quayle cranked it up.

"Where're the life jackets?" shouted Marc above the roar of the motor.

Mr. Quayle waved a careless hand. "They're around. Watch this."

The boat leaped forward. Marc was flung back against the railing. The shores of Slime Lake swept by in a blur.

Marc hated it. His weird sister seemed to like it, though. She kept smiling up at Mr. Quayle and asking him questions. When they reached the Wreck, Mr. Quayle swung the boat in a wide arc and roared up to the far side of the dock. He clicked off the motor.

In the sudden silence, Marc realized that a lot more people had arrived at Slime Lake since their last visit to the Wreck. And that every one of them seemed to be looking at the *Emerald Shores Princess*.

"Look! There's Jaws! And Jordie! And Stacey! And Vickie! And Maria! And Polly Hannah!" said Terri happily.

"Thanks for the ride," mumbled Marc, making his escape while his sister waved at all her friends. He scrambled out of the *Princess*, made his way along the dock to the beach, and sat down next to Jaws and another kid from Graveyard School, Skate McGraw. Jaws was eating a package of peanuts and some ice cream. Skate was staring mournfully out at the flat water.

"How long you here for?" Marc asked Skate.

"A month," said Skate. He didn't sound happy.

But Marc knew it wasn't the changes at Slime Lake that were bothering Skate. It was the lack of skateboarding surface. All the roads around Slime Lake were rutted dirt roads. Skate would have had to go almost all the way back to Grove Hill to find a smooth paved ride.

Jaws said, "They're selling tofu dogs at the recreation stand. I hope my parents don't find out." Jaws's parents were health-food fanatics. As a junk-food consumer, Jaws was in constant fear that they were going to cut off his supply of what they called "nutritionally negative foods."

Marc didn't answer. He watched his sister start talking at top speed to Stacey and Maria, who were best friends, and Jordie and Vickie and even the snobby Polly Hannah.

He yawned.

"Well, I *love* it," he heard Polly say. "It's very neat and clean."

Stacey said, "My father likes to fish. He says that motorboats on this lake are gonna scare off every fish in fifty miles."

"Mr. Quayle is going to drain that nasty swamp, too," said Polly.

Stacey, who liked animals probably more than people and earned extra money as a pet-sitter and dog-walker, said in outrage, "That swamp is an important wildlife habitat."

"Oh, puh-leeze." Polly pushed her dark glasses up and adjusted the pink headband holding her curly hair back. "It's a *swamp*, Stacey."

"Wanna go dive?" Marc asked.

"No. My ice cream will melt," said Jaws.

Skate shrugged. He and Marc got up and walked out on the dock to the diving tower. Marc put on his T-shirt, in case he accidentally did a belly-flop. He knew from past experience that it stung.

Skate already had a T-shirt on. He'd never taken it off and he didn't now. He walked gingerly, as if he wasn't used to going anywhere without wheels beneath his feet.

"Hey! Wait for us!" Terri came hurrying out onto the dock after them. Stacey and Maria were with her.

"I love the diving tower," said Maria.

"Better than Polly, anyway," said Stacey, pretending to gag.

They all looked back at Polly, who was lying flat on her back in the sun, next to Jordie and Vickie. Vickie, who was Skate's cousin, suddenly jumped up and headed for the refreshment stand. Jordie, who was a math whiz, was playing with some kind of computer toy. She probably didn't even know she was sitting by Slime Lake.

But Jordie, like Vickie and most of the other kids, was dressed in comfortable clothes, cutoffs over a faded bathing suit. Her brown hair was pulled back and stuck up under a baseball cap. She looked normal.

Polly looked like a big pink decoration stuck to the sand. She was wearing a bright pink bathing suit. Her towel, which was spread out without a wrinkle beneath her, was spotlessly white with pink trim. She was wearing dark glasses with a pink cord. She had a beach bag, pink of course, sitting next to her, zipped tightly shut. Even her fingernails and toenails were matching pink.

"I'd like to put her in the swamp," said Stacey, beginning to climb up the ladder.

"Or feed her to Emmie," said Skate.

"Me too," said Maria.

Stacey said, "The monster of Emerald Lake. What a stupid idea."

"Yeah. Too bad there isn't a monster in the lake, though," said Maria. She ran her fingers through her short dark hair, making her bangs stick up, as usual.

"Marc thinks there really is a monster," said Terri.

Big thanks to you, sis, thought Marc, feeling his face turn red.

"Yeah?" said Skate.

Trying to sound as if he hadn't just arrived from the Planet Weird, Marc told them what he'd heard the night his sister had gone sleepwalking.

"Cool," said Maria.

"Awesome," said Stacey.

Skate shrugged. He never talked a lot. It was one of the things Marc liked about him.

"We should keep an eye out for it," said Maria. "Maybe we could catch it."

"What for?" asked Terri, frowning.

"Yeah?" said Stacey. "It's not hurting anything."

"It doesn't even exist," said Maria, giving Stacey and Terri an annoyed look. "Chill, okay?"

She walked to the end of the platform and looked down. She took a deep breath and jumped. A moment later they heard her shriek as she hit the water.

"That was *great!*" she shouted up to them. "C'mon!"

Skate leaped up and out and cannonballed into the water.

They dove and swam until it was time for lunch. Then Skate said, "Vickie's waving. I think my aunt and uncle are here to pick us up."

They headed back for the shore. Skate and Vickie left with Vickie's parents. Stacey and Maria and Terri and Marc flopped down on the beach next to Polly.

"Euuw," said Polly. "Quit dripping on me!"

"It's only water, Polly," said Marc.

"Don't get it on my computer," said Jordie. She tucked her computer under her arm and went to sit under one of the trees near the picnic area.

Marc flipped water on Polly. "Stop it!" said Polly angrily. She sat up and pushed up her dark glasses to give Marc a mean look.

"What, you're afraid you'll melt?" snickered Stacey.

Polly included Stacey in her evil look, and Maria and Terri just for good measure.

Then she stopped looking so angry. A sick expression crossed her face. She raised a trembling finger and pointed at Stacey, and then at Maria and Terri and Marc.

"Euuuw! Grooooooosss!"

CHAPTER

6

Stacey looked down. A big green patch of slime was stuck to her bathing suit. Slime was oozing along the shoulder of Marc's T-shirt. It had spread down one side of Maria's bathing suit. And it was actually on Terri's skin.

"Ick!" said Maria, trying to rub the green goo off. "Oh, it's so sticky!"

"It looks like someone yakked on you," said Polly. She clapped her hand over her mouth as if she were about to throw up herself. "It stinks, too."

Terri picked up her towel and began wiping off her leg.

Stacey picked up her towel and rubbed at the hip of her bathing suit. The slime mushed into the faded red material and made a big, ugly stain.

"Great, now I'm going to have to wash it," she said.

Marc had an idea. He bent down and gathered up a handful of sand and rubbed it into the slime on his shirt. The slime stuck to the grains of sand, and the grains of sand stuck to each other and fell to the ground in green, sticky globules.

But the green stain remained.

"We've all been slimed!" said Stacey.

"Why do you think they call it Slime Lake?" cracked Marc.

"Yes, but it's never stuck to anyone like this before," said Stacey. "This is, like, real—goo."

"Real scientific," Maria scoffed at Stacey. "Goo."

Jaws returned from the snack stand holding a large Coke. "Thirsty, anyone?" he said. Then his eye fell on the slime.

"You got that slime on you, huh?" He nodded wisely.

"What do you know about it?" Terri demanded.

"Well, I've been coming here every day all summer and I was the first one here," said Jaws. "I was practically the only one here for a while."

"So?" said Maria.

"So I saw Tiffany scrubbing slime off the dock and the boats one morning. She told me it was part of her job. She has to get here early and do a slime patrol *every* morning. Mr. Quayle doesn't want people to know about the Slime Problem."

"What Slime Problem?" Marc said.

"Some kind of weird algae or something." Jaws took a sip of his Coke. "It's been growing on the lake all summer and it's getting worse and nothing Mr. Quayle can do seems to be stopping it."

"As soon as he drains the swamp, the slime will go away," said Polly, sliding her sunglasses into place and arranging herself carefully on her towel again.

"No it won't!" said Terri, her green eyes flashing.

"No way," agreed Stacey. "I'll tell you what caused the Slime Problem, Polly. Something's upset the natural balance of the lake, and the slime is the result."

Marc looked up toward the concession stand and Mr. Quayle's office. "Gee," he said sarcastically. "I wonder what could be causing the problem!"

A shadow fell across their towels. They looked up.

Tiffany Quayle was standing there with a clipboard in her hand. "How come you never rent any of the boats?" she said. She pointed at the line of canoes on the other side of the dock.

"We have a rowboat," said Marc.

"We just got here," said Maria. "Give us a break, okay?"

"Mr. Quayle is very concerned that people are not renting *his* boats. And that they bring their own picnics to the recreation area instead of buying food at the concession stand."

"But you don't have to buy food at the concession stand or rent canoes to use the recreation area," Terri pointed out.

Tiffany scowled. Then she handed Terri a pen and a clipboard with a piece of paper attached. "Sign here," she ordered.

"Why?" Terri studied the sheet of paper. "It's for a canoe race this Saturday. Why would I want to be in a canoe race?"

"Because it's fun," said Tiffany flatly. She looked up as another shadow fell across the group. "Hello, Uncle George," she said sweetly.

"Hello, Mr. Quayle," said Terri.

"Call me George, call me George. How many times do I have to tell you?" said Mr. Quayle with a big-toothed smile. "Signing up for the canoe race, girls and boys?"

"No," said Marc.

"What's the prize?" asked Maria.

"I haven't decided yet. But it'll be big! Very

big . . . er, you'll probably want to rent a canoe and practice before the race."

Terri grabbed the clipboard and signed. Then she said, "I'm signing you up to be my partner, Marc."

"Wait!" said Marc. But it was too late.

Stacey and Maria signed up. Then Jaws signed up and added Jordie's name as his partner. Stacey took the clipboard and signed up Skate and Vickie. "I'm not getting stuck doing this by myself," she explained.

"Excellent, excellent," said Mr. Quayle, rubbing his hands together in a way that reminded Marc of their oozy assistant principal back at Graveyard School.

When they'd all signed up, Mr. Quayle left, but not before encouraging them to come buy some lunch at the snack stand. Tiffany wandered off in search of more victims for the canoe race.

"Who died and left him king of the lake?" said Maria after Mr. Quayle had left.

"I guess Pops must've sold the Wreck to Mr. Quayle," said Terri. But she didn't sound convinced.

"I can't believe we have to walk home," complained Marc.

"You could've called Uncle Nicholas and asked him to come pick us up," Terri said.

Since they both knew that neither of them would have dared to call their uncle except in an extreme emergency, Terri's argument silenced Marc.

But only for a moment.

"We should have brought our bikes," Marc said.

"These roads would kill our bicycles," said Terri practically.

"True," said Marc.

They walked on. They'd been coming to Slime Lake their whole lives. Following the right trail through the maze of trails that surrounded the lake was second nature.

And Marc had to admit, it wasn't such a bad walk. The lake, which could be seen from the trail, was still in the late-afternoon sun. Dragonflies flitted lazily near the surface of the water. A turtle slid off a flat rock into the water as they walked by.

Sometimes the trail doubled back to skirt someone's property and went along one of the dirt roads. The roads were scarcely bigger than the trail, narrow and deeply rutted, and impassable after every hard rain.

"This place is, like, the end of the world," said Marc.

"Yeah. It's great," said Terri.

They trudged on.

They were almost home when Marc noticed it. He noticed it because of a horsefly. A huge, stinging horsefly that landed on his bare shoulder and took a huge bite out of it.

Marc swatted the fly and missed it. His hand connected with bare skin instead. "Owww!" he cried.

Then he realized what had happened. He looked at his shoulder. It was bare. Where his T-shirt had been was just a big, ragged hole. The edges of the hole were lined with faint traces of green slime.

He stopped. "Terri?" he said.

"What?" She turned.

He pointed to his shoulder. "There's a hole in my T-shirt," he said.

"So?" said Terri. Then her eyes widened. "That's where the slime was!"

"Duh," said Marc.

"It *ate* your shirt!" Terri shrieked. She bent over and began to hop on one leg, slapping at her other leg. *"Oooh, oooh, oooh,"* she moaned. "Get off me!"

Marc yanked the shirt off over his head. He half expected to see that his shoulder was turning into slime-eaten Swiss cheese.

But it wasn't.

"Terri, chill," he said. "It's just chowing down on our clothes." A sudden funny thought struck him. "Won't Polly be ticked when she finds out what this does to all her perfect clothes?"

Terri stopped hopping. She gave her leg one last look. Then she straightened up and began to grin. "Polly the fashion victim," she said.

They both cracked up.

Terri stopped laughing first.

"But it's not really funny, you know," she said. "I mean, something is going on at Slime Lake. Something's wrong."

Marc thought about the monster noise he'd heard. About the toxic slime. About Mr. Quayle and his huge boats and horrible plans. About how Pops had just disappeared.

"Tell me about it," he said. Then he glared at Terri. "You don't have to be so nice to Quayle, you know. What is it—you want to be elected Miss Slime Lake, or something?"

Terri made a face. But she didn't answer. She just said, "Come on. Let's hurry. I want to get home and take a bath and make sure all the slime is gone. I'd hate to wake up in the middle of the night with one leg missing!"

* * *

The house was quiet. Marc got up and went to the window of his room. The moon was brighter now. He could see the dock and the water more clearly.

The lake was as still as glass. The reflection of the moon was mirrored on the still surface.

Uncle Nicholas hadn't had any problems with the mutant cloth-eating slime.

"Ha," was all he'd said when they told their story over dinner.

"I'm glad it eats clothes and not skin," Terri had said. "But it's probably hard on the boats and the docks."

"Ha," Uncle Nicholas had said again. "Not mine."

He'd chewed fiercely for a moment, then looked at Terri. "You don't need to worry," he'd said gruffly.

Terri had smiled back. "Okay," she'd said simply.

Marc pressed his forehead against the screen. Sometimes his sister was such a simp. He went back to bed and lay down.

Something bit him on the shoulder.

He slapped at it. Was there a hole in the screen? Had a mosquito gotten in?

He hated mosquitoes worse than horseflies. Mosquitoes were like ticks with wings—insect vampires. Maybe he should get up and put a shirt on.

It bit him again on the shoulder.

He slapped at it hard.

His hand sank into the soft, dissolving flesh.

For a moment Marc couldn't move. Then he jerked his hand back. It felt as if he were pulling it out of glue.

He bolted upright in the bed. He reached over and touched his shoulder again. Softly. Carefully.

His finger sank into the skin. It touched bone.

"Arrrgh!" Marc sprang from his bed and turned on the light. He stumbled over to the mirror on the back of the closet door.

His face stared back, his eyes wild.

He raised his hand and slapped his face. It stung. It hurt.

It didn't stick. And it proved he wasn't dreaming.

He allowed his gaze to drop to his shoulder.

But it didn't look like his shoulder anymore. His skin was melting away like rotting ice cream, oozing and dripping away from where the slime had touched him.

CHAPTER
7

He screamed.

The door of his room flew open. His sister was standing there.

Below her knee, where the slime had touched her leg, was glistening bone.

"Aaaaaaah!"

Marc screamed again.

A hand grabbed his shoulder.

"Don't touch it, don't touch it!" he cried.

"Marc? Marc, wake up!"

Marc opened his eyes. He was sitting up in his bed. His sister was standing beside him.

"You're having a bad dream."

Throwing off the covers and pushing her aside, Marc charged across the room to the mirror. His shoulder was still there. With a trembling finger, he poked the skin. It stayed firm.

He spun around and stared at Terri's leg. It looked normal.

"Marc?"

"I had a bad dream," Marc said. "A really, really *bad* dream." He told Terri about the flesh-eating slime.

She was impressed, he could tell. "But it couldn't really happen, you know," she said when he finished. "It was just a nightmare."

"I know," he said. But he kept the light beside his bed on for a long time after she left.

Maybe it was a good thing Mr. Quayle wanted to drain the lake. Maybe that would clear up whatever was going wrong.

Because Marc knew for certain now that something was wrong at Slime Lake. And that the trouble was only beginning.

Marc was sulking. He was sulking because his sister, the Mouth of Slime Lake, had told everybody about his nightmare.

And now they all thought he was afraid to go in the water.

Marc flopped back on the planks in the sun. *Maybe I'll just stay here for the rest of the summer,* he thought.

"Hey, Marc, come on in. The water's fine here,"

called Maria. "It was a good idea to swim by your uncle's instead of over by Emerald Shores, or whatever it's called."

"Yeah! No slime!" added Stacey.

Marc raised his head and gave his sister an evil look. He couldn't believe she'd told Stacey and Maria about his nightmare.

"Won't you ever go in the water again?" asked Terri. "It's just slime."

"Mutant slime," muttered Marc. More loudly he said, "I'm not afraid."

"Then why don't you come swimming?"

"There really isn't any slime," Maria added reassuringly.

"I'm not afraid," Marc practically shouted. Forgetting that he really *was* afraid, he sat up and stripped off his T-shirt and his deck shoes. Then he jumped into the water.

The cold made him gasp. But he had to admit, the water felt good. He let himself sink far, far, below the cool green surface. He opened his eyes.

Nearby he could see a pair of long bare legs dangling below the edge of a float. They looked strange and green in the watery light.

With a frog kick he propelled himself to the surface. He shot up like a porpoise and lunged at Stacey. "You're it!" he shouted.

They played tag until it was time for lunch. Afterward they hung out on the dock until they could go swimming again.

"Let's get out the water basketball set," Terri suggested.

"Cool," said Maria.

"I don't know." Stacey yawned. "Maybe we could just sleep in the sun."

"You're going to fry in the sun," said Maria.

"Nope. I have a ton of sunblock on," said Stacey.

"Oh. You're what I smell," said Marc.

"Ha, ha," said Stacey.

Just then Skate came walking down the path and onto the dock.

"Hey!" Terri sat up and waved.

"Hi," said Skate.

"Where's Vickie?" asked Terri.

"At the Wreck, practicing for the canoe race."

"Want to play some water basketball?"

Skate nodded. As Terri spoke he was already pulling off the T-shirt he was wearing with his cutoffs.

Terri jumped up and ran back to the house to get the water basketball set.

"Is everybody at the Wreck?" asked Stacey.

Skate nodded again.

"Like who?" asked Maria.

"Polly. Jaws. Jordie. Tyson and his family just got

here. They're having a picnic at the Wreck. Mr. Quayle got Tyson to sign up for the canoe race, too. Then Tyson told Mr. Quayle that he had his own canoe." Skate shook his head. "Man wasn't happy."

Marc yawned so hard his jaws almost cracked. He hadn't been sleeping well lately, that was true. He propped his hands on his chin and stared out at the lake.

The water was as green as a baseball diamond in the spring. It looked nice and cool and not threatening at all. Waves lapped gently against the pilings of the dock, and the boat pulled gently on its creaking rope. The sky was blue and cloudless.

It was a perfect day.

Marc leaned over the edge of the dock. "Watch out for snakes," he said to Maria.

Maria rolled her eyes and dove under.

Terri came back with the water basketball set, and they teamed up, Marc and Skate against Maria and Terri and Stacey. It was a killer game, cheating allowed. Maria yanked Marc down by a loop on his cutoffs and dunked a basket. Skate splashed Stacey and sunk one over her while she was temporarily blinded. They played until they were gasping for air.

"Final point!" called Marc. He swam out to the edge of the milling players.

Stacey lunged toward him and stole the ball.

"Over here!" shouted Terri, holding up her hand to show she was free.

Skate dove for Stacey, and she ducked to one side. She threw the ball to Terri. It skidded just out of Terri's reach, and Maria scooped it up.

"Got i—" Maria never finished her sentence.

She just disappeared beneath the surface of Slime Lake.

One minute she was there, and the next minute she was gone.

All that remained was the basketball, bobbing gently on the water.

CHAPTER

8

"Maria!" shouted Terri. "Maria!"

"It's a joke," Stacey said.

"It's not a joke," said Marc. Hardly knowing what he was doing, he began to swim to the place where Maria had disappeared. He dove.

The water was a swirl of dark green. He couldn't see anything. But he felt a current of colder water brush past his face.

A face appeared.

"Arrggh," he gurgled. He kicked to the surface.

Stacey surfaced beside him.

"W-What'dja do that for!" he sputtered.

"Sorry," said Stacey. "I didn't mean to scare you."

"She's been under too long for it to be a joke," said Terri frantically. "What'll we do? We've got to do something!"

Marc looked around desperately. He didn't know what to do.

Terri swam to the ladder and flung herself up it. She was halfway up the dock when she stopped and spun around. She shaded her eyes and peered out across the lake.

"Did you hear that?" she cried.

"What?" Stacey asked, her voice sharp with fear.

"Maria!" Terri cried. She cupped her hands around her mouth. "Maria!" she called. "Maria!"

A faint, hoarse cry answered.

"Maria, Maria, it's Maria!" Terri ran back down the dock and jumped into the rowboat. As she untied it and pushed off, Marc flung his leg over the side and pulled himself in.

Together they rowed out to where Maria was thrashing feebly in the water.

"Help me," she gasped. "Help me. . . ."

Terri stuck out her oar, and Maria grabbed it. Using the oar, Terri brought Maria up beside the rowboat. Together she and Marc dragged Maria in.

Maria rolled over the edge of the boat and fell to the floorboards, choking and coughing.

"What happened?" said Marc.

"Let her rest, Marc," said Terri.

Maria shook her head. "N-No. No, I'm okay." Shakily she sat up.

The twins began to row back to the dock. Maria said, "I don't know what happened. One minute I was going up for the ball and the next minute I was being dragged through the water."

"Undertow?" said Marc, remembering the cold current of water that had brushed by him.

"I don't know." Maria coughed. The color was coming back to her face, and she was breathing more normally. "It felt like something grabbed me. Like a hand."

She looked from Terri to Marc. "I thought it was one of you guys. But then when it pulled me through the water so fast, I knew it couldn't be."

They reached the dock. Maria had begun to shiver. Quickly they helped her out of the boat and up onto the dock. She sat down heavily. Stacey helped her pull her T-shirt on over her bathing suit, then wrapped a towel around her shoulders.

"It's okay," said Stacey. "Whatever happened, it's okay."

Maria looked around at the circle of worried faces. "But what was it?" she cried. "Something grabbed me and pulled me under and dragged me through the water. And then it let me go. . . ."

A gruff voice said, "Are you all right? You're not hurt?"

"Uncle Nicholas!" cried Terri.

Marc stared at his uncle in surprise. Uncle Nicholas hardly ever came out onto the dock. He never seemed to go near the lake at all. Sometimes Marc wondered why his uncle even lived there.

"Something pulled Maria under the water, Uncle Nicholas," said Terri. "What could it have been?"

Uncle Nicholas didn't answer Terri. Instead he said to Maria, "How did you get pulled under? Did something bite you?"

"My ankle." Maria pointed. "Something grabbed my ankle."

Uncle Nicholas bent over and looked at Maria's ankle. A faint red mark could be seen, nothing more. And the mark was fading rapidly.

Uncle Nicholas nodded and straightened. "You ought to be careful, swimming in the lake."

"We are careful," said Marc. He moved around to stare up at his uncle. "We weren't doing *anything*. Just playing basketball."

Turning away, Uncle Nicholas said, "An undertow, most likely. An underground stream, coming up from the bottom. Lake's full of 'em."

He looked over his shoulder. "Full of underground caves, too. You could get pulled under and never come up."

"Uncle Nicholas," said Marc.

"Just be careful!" their uncle roared. "That's all I'm saying. Be very careful!" He stomped back up the dock and disappeared along the path.

Marc looked down at Maria's ankle. Then he looked out at the lake. Underground caves? Monsters? It wasn't possible.

Was it?

No one wanted to go back in the water.

"Maybe it was a shark," said Stacey. "I read about a shark that swam up this river from the ocean and ate this kid who was diving off a dock into the river."

"If it was a shark, Maria wouldn't have a leg," said Marc. "Just a bloody stump with bloody giant tooth-marks and—"

"Could we not talk about this?" Maria said.

"Sorry," said Stacey.

"Maybe it really was an undertow," said Terri. "Or some kind of seaweed."

"It pulled Maria halfway to the middle of the lake," said Marc. "How could seaweed do that? Unless that slime really has become, like, mutant ninja slime."

"She got caught on it, it got caught in the undertow, that's how," said Terri.

"Maybe," said Skate. But he didn't sound convinced.

*   *   *

Marc wasn't convinced either. And he didn't think his sister believed her own explanation.

"Weird. Beyond weird," he said.

He and Terri were sitting on the end of the dock—the end closest to shore. They were watching the sun go down. Soon it would be dark. Bats swooped in the shadows, eating insects. A bird skimmed the water of the lake, then disappeared into the marsh. It grew cooler.

Marc said, "Think about it. Something was howling that night you were sleepwalking. It tried to knock over the dock—maybe to grab you and me. . . ."

His sister didn't look at him. But he knew she was listening intently.

"Then this slime starts attacking things on the lake, eating away the paint on boats and the pilings of piers and even our clothes.

"And then this. Something grabs Maria and pulls her under."

Terri glanced sideways at her brother. "You were imagining things, that night I was sleepwalking. The slime is caused by acid rain. Look what acid rain does to the trees! And Maria got pulled under by some lake-weed and an undertow."

"You don't really believe that, do you?" asked Marc.

"No," said Terri.

She turned to face her brother. "I think there's a monster in Slime Lake, that's what I think. Not a cute monster named Emmie but a real live monster. Living down there in one of the caves."

"We'd better hurry, Marc." Terri interrupted his thoughts. "Or we'll miss the canoe race."

"Fine by me," said Marc.

"You want to walk or take the rowboat?"

"Walk," said Marc quickly. "We have to save our arms for the paddling in the race."

He didn't say he didn't want to take the rowboat out on the lake. Not now or ever again.

"We're going to walk over to the Wreck for the canoe race, Uncle Nicholas!" Terri called back into the depths of the old house.

No one answered. As usual.

Marc wondered if Uncle Nicholas was even home. And what did their uncle do all day, anyway?

Uncle Nicholas hadn't mentioned again what had happened to Maria. But Marc had caught their uncle staring at Terri and at him more than once at dinner that night.

Marc wondered if any of the other kids had told their parents. He knew he and Terri weren't going to.

"Too weird," Skate had said when Marc asked him after they'd reached the Wreck.

Maria had said, "Maybe it *was* the undertow . . . and if it was, and I told my parents, they'd probably never let me go in the water again or something."

Stacey had nodded.

Vickie had shrugged, borrowing Skate's usual response to everything. More than anything, she was clearly annoyed that she hadn't been there.

Now Marc let his gaze roam over the crowd. It was a pretty big turnout. All the picnic tables were filled, and some people had even spread blankets on the ground. Although most people had brought their own picnics, the concession stand was doing a brisk business. Meanwhile, Tiffany was stretching a nylon cord from the outside edge of the dock, across the water in front of the shore where the canoes were drawn up onto the beach, to a buoy anchored in the water. The cord was hung with flags and was suspended about three feet above the surface.

The sound of a trumpet playing reveille blasted over the loudspeakers above the concession stand.

Half the people who were gathered clapped their hands over their ears. Silence fell.

The trumpet ceased abruptly. Then Mr. Quayle bounded through the picnickers and over to the canoes where the contestants were waiting. He signaled to Tiffany, who sullenly blew a shrill blast on her whistle.

"Boys and girls, ladies and gentlemen, honored guests, future members of the Emerald Shores Country Club . . ."

"Country club?" whispered Terri. "There's no country club here!"

"There will be if Mr. Quayle has his way," Marc whispered back.

Mr. Quayle was rambling on. ". . . the first of many fine Emerald Shores recreational events. Soon we will have regattas. Jet Ski water barrel racing. Maybe even speedboat races . . ."

"What about the no motors on the lake rule?" someone in the crowd called.

Mr. Quayle squinted in the direction of the voice. He looked distinctly less friendly for a moment. But he kept his voice smooth. "Rules can be changed."

Murmurs swept through the audience.

Mr. Quayle continued hastily, "But on to the event at hand—the first annual Emerald Shores Recreation Center Canoe Race for Kids! The starting line, which is that row of flags out by the end of the dock, is also the finish line. You will row out to the striped green-and-white buoy in the middle of the lake and around it and then back to the flags. The first canoe under the flags wins. Any questions?"

"Yeah," said Marc. "What's the prize?"

Mr. Quayle gave Marc an annoyed look. "It's a surprise," he said.

"I bet it is," Marc muttered.

"Okay, everyone, life jackets on? Okay! To your canoes. And may the best canoe win!"

Everyone ran to jump into the canoes and paddle them out to the starting line.

Terri and Marc pulled up between Jaws and Jordie and Stacey and Maria.

Jaws was eating an ice cream cone. Jordie was playing a computer game.

But Stacey and Maria looked ready to paddle. They were wearing matching baseball hats pulled low on their foreheads. They even had sunglasses on.

When they were all lined up, more or less, Mr. Quayle said, "Ready? Set? *Go!*"

Marc and Terri began to paddle at top speed. They quickly passed Jaws and Jordie. They pulled neck and neck with Vickie and Skate.

"Ha!" said Vickie. "Forget it!" She began to paddle even more furiously. Suddenly the paddle slipped out of her hands. "Nooo!" she cried and lunged sideways to grab it. The canoe almost tipped over.

"Ha, *ha,*" said Marc meanly as they shot by.

They passed Tyson and his partner. Soon they

were neck and neck with the leaders, including Stacey and Maria. As they approached the turn around the buoy, Stacey looked over her shoulder. She said something to Maria, and the two girls turned their canoe directly across the path of Terri and Marc's canoe.

"Look out!" shouted Terri. She and Mark paddled backward frantically.

"Watch where you're going!" shouted Vickie behind them.

They swung wide, narrowly missing Vickie and Skate as they raced by.

"No fair," panted Terri as the nose of their canoe swung out to point toward the far shore of the lake.

"All's fair in canoe race," shouted Stacey. She dug her paddle deep into the water.

Stacey's canoe tilted.

"Be careful!" shouted Maria.

Stacey tugged at her paddle. She leaned back. She pulled with all her might.

The paddle suddenly popped out of the water.

Stacey flailed backward. Her canoe bobbed and tilted like a crazy cork.

"Watch *out*!" shouted Vickie. She dug her own paddle into the water, then straightened up, her eyes widening.

Stacey had raised her own dripping paddle to inspect it. Only it didn't look like a paddle anymore. It looked like a big slime-green cookie with a big bite taken out of it.

Leaving only enormous tooth marks behind.

CHAPTER

9

Someone screamed.

Vickie tried to turn her canoe to help Stacey.

But the water suddenly seemed to boil and heave, and Vickie and Skate's canoe began to spin around and around.

"Help!" shouted Stacey.

"Help!" shouted Vickie.

Skate kept paddling, his teeth clenched, his knuckles white.

"Eeeeeeeh!" screamed Maria.

People onshore had begun to scream. Marc had a confused impression of whistles blowing and people running and pointing.

"Marc, watch out!" Marc looked up and at the last minute managed to paddle out of the way of Skate and Vickie's wildly spinning canoe.

"Help!" shouted Vickie.

The water heaved and shuddered beneath them like the skin of a gigantic animal. Skate and Vickie and Stacey and Maria had abandoned all attempts to paddle and were holding on to the sides of their canoes with all their might. The other canoers who'd been behind them had turned their canoes around and were paddling toward shore for their lives.

Suddenly something hit the bottom of Marc and Terri's canoe.

Marc thought he saw an enormous eye peering up at him from just below the surface of the water.

Then their canoe jolted upward again.

"Marc!" screamed Terri. "Marc, watch out!"

Marc felt himself flying upward into the air. The next thing he knew, he had landed in the churning, monster-maddened waters of the lake.

His life jacket helped him power to the surface. He saw Terri's face, her eyes blazing with excitement. She pointed. She said something he didn't understand.

Marc lunged for the canoe. Just as he did, it spun away.

He felt a terrific surge of water. Something brushed his leg.

He screamed uncontrollably.

The canoe leaped once more into the air. It seemed

to hang above the lake, with Terri clutching the side. Then it fell, and Terri sailed out.

She and the canoe hit the water at the same time, with an enormous splash. This time the canoe landed upside down.

Swimming toward it, Marc shouted, "Terri! Terri!" But he doubted she could hear him above all the noise.

Something hit him in the head.

He ducked.

"Grab the paddle!" Skate shouted practically in his ear. *"Get out of the water."*

With Skate and Vickie's help, Marc heaved himself over the edge of their canoe, half filling it with water.

"Terri," he choked out. "We've got to help Terri."

"Marc, it's okay. She's okay," said Vickie. She pointed.

Terri was clinging to the side of the overturned canoe.

The water gave one last mighty surge and then was still. But the chaos continued. Kids thrashed and splashed and fought their way back to shore. Canoes got banged and battered and overturned. Paddles floated away.

Terri held on to their canoe while Marc and Skate and Vickie towed it in to shore. Terri bobbed like a buoy, talking the whole time.

"Awesome!" she cried. "Amazing! Did you see it? Did you?"

"Calm down, everyone," Mr. Quayle was calling, striding up and down. "An unfortunate accident. No one was hurt. . . . "

"Accident!" shouted Stacey. She held up her half-eaten paddle. "You call this an accident!"

"It was the monster!" Terri said suddenly. "The Slime Lake Monster. She's—"

"Free sodas and snacks for everyone at the snack bar!" Mr. Quayle bellowed, drowning them both out.

What a bunch of lemmings, thought Marc in disgust as the crowd turned toward the snack bar.

Mr. Quayle stormed over to Terri and Stacey and grabbed each of them by an arm.

"Ow!" said Terri. "Let go."

"Let go or I'll sue you," snarled Stacey.

Mr. Quayle let them go. He snatched the paddle out of Stacey's hand.

"Hey!"

"There is *no* monster," he said. "Slime Lake doesn't exist anymore and there is no monster. This"—he held up the paddle and gestured furiously—"is just some trick to scare me away. Well, it won't work!"

"But I saw it—" Terri began.

Mr. Quayle turned on her so suddenly that she

78

jumped back. His eyes blazing, he said, "A trick! Trying to ruin me. And I know who put you up to it, too, young lady. That uncle of yours. Well, wait till I'm through with him. I'll make him sorry he was ever born!"

With that Mr. Quayle marched away.

"He seemed kinda upset," said Skate.

"Do you think there really is a monster in the lake?" asked Maria.

No one answered her. But Terri, who had been staring after Mr. Quayle, suddenly said, "I hope so."

"What? Are you crazy?" said Vickie.

"No," said Terri softly. "But what if there isn't a monster? What if it's Uncle Nicholas doing all these things, like Mr. Quayle said?"

But when Terri and Marc told their uncle what had happened, they didn't get the reaction they expected.

Uncle Nicholas, who'd been mending one of the oarlocks on the rowboat, stared fiercely at them. Then an unfamiliar expression appeared on his face.

"Uncle Nicholas! Are you all right?" cried Terri.

Uncle Nicholas coughed and wheezed like a long-unused car being cranked up. Then he began to laugh.

"Ha, ha, ha," he wheezed. "Ha, ha. Is George Quayle calling *me* a monster? That's a good one! Ha, ha, ha."

"Are you doing those things, Uncle Nicholas?" demanded Marc.

As quickly as he'd begun to laugh, Uncle Nicholas stopped. He stared into Marc's eyes. "What do you think? Think I swam under the water and bit that paddle in half?"

"I saw it," said Terri suddenly. "I saw a big head and a big eye, like the eye of a seal. . . ."

Marc suddenly remembered the eye he'd seen. And the thing that had brushed against his leg in the churning water in the middle of the canoe race.

"Are you saying there really is a monster, Uncle Nicholas?" asked Marc. "Is that what you're saying?"

Uncle Nicholas bent over and tightened the oarlock. "There now," he said, as much to himself as to anyone. "Fixed."

"Uncle Nicholas?" said Terri.

"Unless, of course, the monster comes along and eats it." Uncle Nicholas put his tools in his toolbox and stood up. He walked back up the dock and disappeared into the shade of the trees surrounding his house.

There was a note stuck to the refrigerator that night: "You're on your own for dinner. Help yourselves."

"Cool," said Marc. "Let's send out for pizza."

Terri rolled her eyes at him.

"Just a joke," Marc said. "So if a monster is famous, what do you call it? A mon-star. Get it? Star."

"Marc. Puh-leeze." Terri opened the freezer door. "There's frozen pizza."

"Sail it over," said Marc. "I'll stick it in the oven."

"We should eat a vegetable or something, too, shouldn't we?"

"You sound like Polly Hannah," Marc scoffed. He made a face. "Besides, I swallowed enough green slime today in the lake to put me off green food forever."

"Maybe it's not slime," said Terri slyly. "Maybe it's monster poop. You know, like when fish go in aquariums."

Marc truly did think he was going to hurl. Not that he'd give Terri the satisfaction of knowing it.

He managed to eat his pizza anyway. "I wonder what monsters really do eat. Besides people, I mean. Do they like anchovies?"

His sister made a face. Then she said thoughtfully, "Maybe they don't eat people. You know, like, whales are enormous and they don't eat people. Just fish and plankton or something."

"Killer whales eat people," said Marc.

"That's different," Terri argued. "That's just one whale, and besides, it's a whole different part of the whale family, or something."

Marc shrugged. He was tired of thinking about monsters. He personally planned on never setting foot in Slime Lake again. Because he wanted to keep his foot.

Hadn't Terri seen the size of the tooth marks in Stacey's paddle?

"The monster could have bitten me, or you, instead of the paddle," said Terri, as if she were reading Marc's thoughts. "But it didn't. I mean, maybe there's nothing to be afraid of."

Marc put down his slice of pizza. His sister was from another planet. His completely out-of-it sister.

His sister who believed in monsters.

Nice monsters.

He leaned over and stared his sister in the eyes. "Be afraid," he told her. "Be very, very afraid."

CHAPTER
10

The air was very, very still. And very, very hot. The sky was an ominous dark blue. The waters of Slime Lake were an ominous dark green.

Terri said, "If I go swimming, maybe we can attract the monster."

"Yeah, right," Marc scoffed. "We'll just use you as live bait. Mom and Dad'll love that. Forget it, Terri."

"I'm roasting. Dying. Meltihg," Terri complained.

"Welcome to the club," answered Marc grouchily.

Ever since the canoe race, Slime Lake had been strangely quiet. No one had come over to see Terri and Marc. They hadn't gone to see anybody else, either.

Nor had they gone back to the Wreck. They knew, somehow, that Mr. Quayle wouldn't exactly welcome them with open arms.

Marc had awakened once, thinking he'd heard the sound of Mr. Quayle's motorboat out on the lake in the night. But what would the motorboat be doing at the swamp end of the lake in the middle of the night? He hadn't gone to the window to check it out.

He didn't know what he'd see out on that cold, dark lake.

And he hated surprises.

Whatever Marc had heard, by day the lake was dead. He looked now up toward the Wreck. Nothing. No canoers. No swimmers. No sailboats.

No motorboat.

Not a sign of life anywhere.

Everyone's lying low, thought Marc. *Waiting to see what will happen next.*

Maybe Mr. Quayle *would* be glad to see them. Business was probably terrible. On that thought, Marc yawned so hard his jaws cracked.

"I'm going swimming," Terri announced.

"You can't," said Marc. "Even if you could you can't, because you just ate lunch and you have to wait for an hour." He yawned again.

"Will you quit yawning? You're making me yawn, too."

Marc yawned in Terri's face.

"You're a pig, Marc Foster," said Terri. She rolled over on her stomach on her towel and closed her eyes.

Marc yawned again and lay down on his towel. He flipped open his comic book.

And fell asleep.

When he woke up, the sun was going down.

The ripples from the splash in the water at the end of the dock were spreading in perfect, menacing circles.

"Terri!" He bolted upright.

His crazy sister was treading water near the end of the dock.

"Get out of the water, Terri," he said.

For an answer, she dove beneath the surface. She came up with her hair slicked back like a seal's.

"Come on, Marc. It's fine."

Far out in the lake, near the swamp, his eye caught a faint swell of water.

Just a breeze, he told himself. *Just a breeze.*

But he knew it wasn't. Not a breath of air was stirring.

"Get out of the water, Terri."

"Chicken," said Terri, and dove down again.

Great, thought Marc. He could see the headline now: Girl Eaten by Monster While Twin Brother Just Watches.

Terri resurfaced farther out.

"Terri!" he said. The swell of water was closer. Only

now it looked more like water sliding off something as it glided just beneath the surface of the water.

Was that a flipper he saw? A *fin*?

"Terri, it's behind you," he said desperately, trying to keep his voice calm. He began to lower himself one rung at a time down the ladder.

"Sure," she said. "Is it big? Green? Does it have long, pointed teeth?"

Marc looked up from the ladder.

His eyes widened. "Y-e-e-e-ss!" he screamed.

Terri turned.

Her mouth dropped open, but she never got to scream.

Something pulled her under in one quick, smooth motion. Then the lake was still.

"Terri!" Marc shouted, and half jumped, half fell into Slime Lake.

Something smelled awful.

Marc opened his eyes carefully. It was too dark to see anything. His eyelids were sticking together. His face was sticky.

Blood, he thought. *I'm covered in blood.*

I'm dying. I've been half eaten, like the paddle, and the rest of me left behind for a snack.

Chill, Foster, he told himself. *This is a dream. Like the slime dream.*

Like Terri's nightmare, only worse.

He sat up. As he did, he realized that he had all his fingers and toes, both his arms and both his legs.

And he wasn't covered with blood. He recognized that smell.

He was covered with slime.

He wasn't the only thing in the darkness that was covered with slime. He put his hand out and felt cold, damp rock—and slime.

Where was he? How had he gotten there? The last thing he remembered was falling into the lake.

No, the last thing he remembered was falling into the lake and coming face-to-face with:

The monster.

One enormous eye, peering through the green boiling water into his.

So I fainted a little bit, thought Marc. *No, I played dead. That's it. I played dead and the monster brought me back to his cave to eat later.*

Smart move, Foster.

Because, of course, that was where he was. Had to be. He could almost hear Uncle Nicholas's voice telling them about the caves beneath the lake.

The monster had caught him and brought him home for dinner.

But where was Terri?

He opened his mouth to call, then thought better

of it. What if the monster was sleeping nearby?

Marc strained his ears and eyes in the darkness. He held his breath and concentrated.

All he could hear was the beating of his own heart.

"Terri?" he whispered. The whisper floated through a huge darkness with a faint echo. No one answered.

He cleared his throat. "Terri?"

"Territerriterri," the echo came back mockingly.

He was in a cave. A pretty big cave by the sound of it.

I have to get out of here, he thought. *I have to find Terri. I have to find the way out.*

But what if the monster was guarding the entrance? What if this was just one of millions of caves and he was trapped forever? What if this was some sort of monster game called Hunt the Kid in the Caves?

Stop that, he told himself. *First you try to escape, then you get eaten. There's plenty of time for panic.*

He got stiffly to his knees. He stretched his hands out over his head. Nothing.

He got to his feet.

He hoped the slime didn't eat his shorts.

Either the cave was huge or Marc was going in circles. He couldn't tell how long he'd been groping along the rough, cold, slimy walls with the palms of his hands, but it seemed like forever.

Then he stepped in something wet.

Water, he told himself as he jumped back with a stifled scream. *It's just water.*

It was just water. And above the water, his hands met nothing at all. He'd found the entrance to the cave.

Cautiously Marc waded forward. The water sloshed around his feet. It had a distinctly slimy feel.

He kept going, keeping one hand on the wall, the other out and to the side so that he wouldn't crash into the wall or anything else. The floor beneath his feet began to slope downward.

The water began to rise around his legs. The steeper the floor became, the deeper the water.

His waist. His chest. His chin.

Marc stopped. He put his hand up over his head. Nothing.

The water's going to get deeper, he thought. *The passage out is underwater.*

Could he swim out? Was the passage totally underwater or just half full? If it went deeper and filled all the way up, there was no way he could swim out. He would drown for sure.

Marc took a deep breath. He stepped forward and began to swim. Every few seconds he stopped and stuck his hand out to touch the wall. Then he raised his arm to see if there was still space above his head.

He didn't swim very long. The third time he stopped and raised his arm, his hand hit the ceiling of the passage.

At the same moment he felt the water swell around him as if something big had lowered itself into it. Then the water began to lap against the sides of the cave.

Marc knew what it was. The monster was swimming down the passage. It was coming back for him.

He turned and swam for his life.

He was swimming so fast and furiously that he didn't realize he'd reached the shallow water at the end of the tunnel in the cave until he scraped his knee against rock. Dripping and gasping, he scrambled to his feet.

A huge swell of water rushed past his knees. He heard splashing behind him.

Blindly, his hands outstretched, he ran forward. The water sucked him back. The slime made his slip and slide.

He fell.

And then the monster was on him. Everything went black.

CHAPTER

11

"Marc! Marc!"

Marc opened his eyes. The light made him wince.

He was lying in a pool of water on the floor of a cave in the beam of a flashlight.

And something big and heavy was breathing nearby, like a giant, snuffly-nosed horse.

Marc held up his hand and squinted. "T-Terri? *Uncle Nicholas?*"

"Hi, Marc," said Terri. "Isn't this awesome?"

Marc sat up. "If this is your idea of a stupid joke, Terri Foster . . ."

Uncle Nicholas spoke. "I must apologize. It's not a joke. Quite the contrary."

That stopped Marc for a moment. Uncle Nicholas was apologizing! And if his voice wasn't warm and friendly, at least it wasn't cold and distant, either.

Then something coughed a giant cough in the surrounding darkness and Marc remembered where he was. "What's that?" he demanded. "What's going on?"

"That's Emmie!" said Terri.

Uncle Nicholas made a disapproving sound, but Terri just grinned and went on. "At least, that's what I've been calling her. Uncle Nicholas says it isn't respectful, but I don't think she minds."

As Terri spoke, Uncle Nicholas slowly turned the beam of his powerful flashlight to one side.

Marc saw an enormous flipper, as big as a table. Then he saw a smooth, broad chest and a long, elegant neck. The neck suddenly arched up and then down, and a head came into view.

"*Aaaah!*" shouted Marc in spite of himself.

The head turned toward Marc. It was big and smooth, with a slight crest on top that was folded down. Her eyes were large and seal-like. Her mouth was slightly open, and her nostrils flared as she turned toward Marc. She dipped her head toward him.

"She's welcoming you," said Uncle Nicholas.

Marc held out his hand. Emmie blew out on it once, then lifted her head again. She looked at Uncle Nicholas.

Uncle Nicholas nodded.

"You're in," said Terri. "You passed the test."

"What," said Marc, "is going on?" And then he sneezed.

"We need to get you into some dry clothes. Come on." Uncle Nicholas turned and led the way across the cavern, away from the entrance. In the beam of the flashlight, Marc saw that a rough stone ladder had been carved into the wall. The ladder led up to a narrow hole.

"Up you go," said Uncle Nicholas. "We've got a ways to go before we get to the surface."

Marc looked over his shoulder. The monster stood silently, an enormous shadow behind them.

"Bye, Emmie," called Terri. "See you later."

The shadow ducked her head. Then the water surged up for a moment, and the monster was gone.

"Can someone please tell me what's going on?" said Marc.

He was warm. He was dry. He was sitting in Uncle Nicholas's tower, which, as far as he could tell, was connected to the cave they'd been in by a long series of underground tunnels.

They were on the top floor of the tower, which gave a commanding view of the lake and the edge of the swamp.

Uncle Nicholas answered, "It's simple, really. I'm the Keeper of the Lake. It is a job that is handed down from one generation to another. I inherited the job from my grandmother when she was a very old woman. But of course she began teaching me what I needed to know when I was much younger."

Their uncle paused and shook his head. "The lake has always been here. It is connected, I believe, although I am not certain, to other lakes and rivers and perhaps even to the oceans by underground tunnels and rivers and chains of caves and caverns. I am only familiar with the caverns and tunnels surrounding this lake.

"Emmie is . . ." Uncle Nicholas paused and looked at Terri. "I'll teach you her proper name later and her language, as befits the Keeper of the Lake. Emmie is the spirit of the lake, if you will. She is one of many who come and go, traveling, as I surmise, from other lakes and so forth. However, she is the only one with whom I have direct contact . . ."

Uncle Nicholas's voice trailed off. He walked to the window and pushed the heavy curtain aside to peer out. "Ah," he said. "Time to go back to the swamp."

"But what about—" Marc began.

"I'll tell you as we travel," answered Uncle Nicholas briskly.

"Back!" said Marc. "To the cold and the dark? To those caves?"

"You did quite well in that cave back there." Uncle Nicholas sounded amused. "Come along."

Before Marc could argue, Uncle Nicholas had thrust a flashlight into his hand and one into Terri's. "When I tell you to turn these off, turn them off," he said. "We don't want to give ourselves away too soon."

"But—"

"Come *on,* Marc," said Terri impatiently.

The stone in the floor of the tower lifted up quite easily.

"To make a long story short, for the moment," said Uncle Nicholas as they descended into the caves, "I knew that it was time for me to start teaching my successor. But the fact that you were twins had confused me. At first I thought Terri was the next Keeper, then Marc.

"Emmie, of course, harbored no such doubts. She knew all along that it was both of you.

"Then Pops disappeared and Quayle came along. I didn't know how Quayle persuaded Pops to give him the Wreck, but I was fairly certain it wasn't legal. However, with Pops missing, my hands were tied.

"That's when, er, Emmie stepped in— Shhh!"

Uncle Nicholas stopped.

"Voices," said Terri.

Then Marc heard them, too. Faint, faraway voices.

Uncle Nicholas turned and walked quickly down a narrow side tunnel. They followed the twists and turns, taking several other branches, until he stopped again. "Lights out," he whispered, taking Terri's hand. She reached back and took Marc's.

They turned off their flashlights and stood in darkness. Then Marc felt Terri's hand tug his, and they moved forward.

Somehow—Marc wasn't quite sure how—they emerged suddenly into the still, moonless, starlit night. They stopped.

Faintly and far away, the flickering of light came through the trees. Once again without flashlights, Uncle Nicholas led them forward. It was almost as if he could see in the dark, picking his way across the quivering, quicksand-like swamp.

As they got closer, the flickering light became a pinprick of light coming through the chinks of a rough wooden cabin.

They pushed closer and closer, until they were crouched at one side of the cabin.

"I'm running out of patience," said an angry voice.

Marc's eyes widened. It was Mr. Quayle.

"I'm not," said a calm voice.

It was Pops.

Mr. Quayle laughed. It was an evil sound. "Well, if you won't sign the deed to your property on the lake, then there are other ways of making you cooperate."

The door of the cabin flew open so suddenly that Marc jumped. Mr. Quayle marched out. He jerked on the end of a rope and Pops emerged, his hands tied together. Pops stumbled.

"Don't try to escape," snarled Mr. Quayle. "You won't get far in this swamp with your hands tied."

Pops didn't answer. His head down, he shuffled after Mr. Quayle.

Uncle Nicholas and Marc and Terri followed the two men to a narrow channel of water. The *Emerald Shores Princess* was anchored there.

"On the boat," said Mr. Quayle. He yanked Pops aboard and began pulling up the anchor.

"You won't sign, so you're going to have a little accident," he said. "A simple drowning. You don't have any relatives. So your property will be sold. And I'll be right there to buy it."

Uncle Nicholas suddenly stepped out. "Haven't you forgotten a little detail, Quayle? If Pops has made out a will, then what?"

Mr. Quayle froze. Then his face turned red with fury.

"You!" he shrieked. "You're next!" He swung the anchor over his head and hurled it at Uncle Nicholas.

Uncle Nicholas jumped one way and Terri and Marc jumped the other. The anchor fell between them.

The boat started with a roar.

"You'll never catch me! You can't prove anything! This lake is mine, mine, mine!" shrieked Mr. Quayle. Leaning over, he slashed the anchor rope.

The boat leaped forward and roared down the narrow channel.

Uncle Nicholas began to run. Desperately Marc and Terri ran after him. But they were too late. The boat roared out of the swamp and onto the lake as they reached the edge.

"Whoa!" said Uncle Nicholas.

"He's getting away!" panted Marc. "He's going to kill Pops. . . ."

The boat suddenly shot straight into the air. Marc heard a horrible scream. "No! No! Noooooooo!"

CHAPTER
12

The boat seemed to explode.

They heard one last horrible scream.

And then there was silence.

"Pops!" cried Terri. "Pops is going to drown. His hands are tied!"

She ran forward, but Uncle Nicholas caught her. "Wait."

Then they saw it. In the beams of their flashlights, a gentle swell broke the water. Emmie came swimming toward them, her head lifted just above the water. She had something in her mouth—Pops!

She swept up to the edge of the water and gently lowered Pops to the ground. Then Emmie twisted her neck back and plucked someone else out of the water—Mr. Quayle. She let him fall to the ground with a thud. Then, in a flash of green and gold and purple, she was gone.

"You okay?" Uncle Nicholas said, bending over to cut the rope on Pops's hands.

"Yep," said Pops.

Uncle Nicholas took the rope and expertly wound it around Mr. Quayle's hands. Mr. Quayle was unconscious, but he was breathing.

Pops chuckled. "We'll make sure that when he wakes, he won't be back to Slime Lake."

"I can't believe Mr. Quayle changed his mind and sold the Wreck back to Pops," said Stacey.

"I'm glad he did," said Maria.

"Yeah," added Jaws. "No more health food at the concession stand."

Marc smiled and looked down at the T-shirt he was wearing with a picture of "the Emerald Lake Monster" on it. Beside him, his sister didn't say anything. But he knew what she was thinking.

The Wreck was back to normal. Pops had painted over most of the bright green paint. He'd given away all the Emerald Shores T-shirts and souvenirs. Nothing strange or unusual had happened since Mr. Quayle had just disappeared. The slime was receding. No monsters had been sighted.

Emmie had been responsible for the slime. She'd been waging her own war against Mr. Quayle.

According to Uncle Nicholas, she'd also been trying to get him to realize that both Terri and Marc were Keepers. Terri had sensed it, which was why she hadn't been all that afraid of the whole idea of monsters.

Marc, like Uncle Nicholas, was stubborn. In the end Emmie had kidnapped both Marc and Terri, not only to make her point, but because she'd just discovered where Pops was being hidden, somewhere in the swamp. She moved too slowly on land, even the swampy land that was her second home out of the water, to rescue Pops herself.

Only, in the end, she had rescued him after all.

Twin Keepers. It made sense now, since Uncle Nicholas had no successor.

Marc and Terri had learned a lot already.

"I think she was giving Quayle a hard time at the canoe race," Uncle Nicholas had said. "Although she might have been trying to fix the race in your favor." And he'd actually smiled.

Tyson paddled his canoe up to the shore and waved. "Wanna come out in the canoe?" he called.

Stacey shook her head. "I don't think I'm ready for

that yet." She jumped up. "I'm ready to take a swim. Anybody else want to come?"

Maria looked out over the lake. Skate was jumping off the diving tower. Vickie was splashing around in the water below. Maria looked up at the lifeguard—a new kid, and a pretty nice one.

"Okay," said Maria.

"Come on!" called Tyson, waving his paddle.

Terri jumped up. "I think I will go out in the canoe. Maybe we should get Pops to hold another canoe race."

Polly shuddered and frowned. "Aren't you all afraid of monsters?" she whined.

Halfway to the canoe, Terri stopped and turned. "Monsters?" she said. "There are no monsters in Slime Lake."

Her eyes met Marc's. *Not anymore*, they both thought.

Terri turned back around and ran to jump into the canoe.

Marc leaned back and folded his arms and stared out over the water. It was deep green and calm. Somewhere Emmie, whose real name Marc now knew, swam peacefully beneath the waters of Slime Lake.

I love this lake, thought Marc.

Me too, he heard her answer as she swam by.

Make your own Slime!

Follow this simple recipe, and not only will you have green, goopy slime—you'll have a tasty treat, too!

SLIME LAKE GUACAMOLE

Ingredients:

2 ripe avocados, halved and pitted
4 teaspoons lemon juice
1 large ripe tomato, chopped
1 tablespoon chopped red onion
Dash of Tabasco
Black olives, halved and pitted
Tortilla chips

In a bowl, combine the avocados and lemon juice and mash thoroughly. Then, with a fork, gently mix in the tomato, onion, Tabasco, and salt and pepper to taste. Garnish with the black olives and serve at room temperature with tortilla chips. Refrigerate leftovers.

How to keep your slime green: Save an avocado stone and keep it in the mixture in the refrigerator.

CAMP DRACULA

Tom B Stone

Jeep Holmes doesn't want to go to summer camp – especially not to one called Camp Dracula!

Why do the other kids sleep hanging upside down?
Who put bats in his bunk?
Why won't they share his garlic bread?

Can Jeep grin and bear it – or will he be driven batty?

ALIENS ATE MY HOMEWORK

Bruce Coville

Do you have a problem telling lies? Can you only speak the truth – no matter how silly?

Then you'll know how Rod felt when his teacher asked about his science project – because he could only tell her the truth: 'Aliens ate my homework, Miss Maloney!'

Of course, nobody believes Rod, so nobody bothers to ask where the aliens come from. Just as well – because Rod is helping Madame Pong and the crazy crew of the *Ferkel* on a very secret mission . . .

Another Hodder Children's book

I LEFT MY SNEAKERS IN DIMENSION X

Bruce Coville

Rod's summer holiday is completely ruined!

First, Elspeth his bratty cousin comes to stay – and she won't leave him alone.

Then he's kidnapped by an alien monster and taken to Dimension X (where Rod realises that Elspeth is the least of his problems!).

And then, cranky monsters and furious aliens force Rod to make the most terrifying decision of his life . . .

GRAVEYARD SCHOOL SERIES
Tom B Stone

☐	63693 9	Deadly Dinners	£2.99
☐	63694 7	The Headless Bike Rider	£2.99
☐	63600 9	Wicked Wheels	£2.99
☐	63601 7	Little Pet Werewolf	£2.99
☐	63602 5	Revenge of the Dinosaurs	£2.99
☐	63603 3	Camp Dracula	£2.99
☐	66476 2	Slime Lake	£2.99

ROD ALLBRIGHT SERIES
Bruce Coville

☐	65115 6	Aliens Ate My Homework	£2.99
☐	65116 4	I Left My Sneakers in Dimension X	£2.99
☐	65355 8	Aliens Stole My Dad	£2.99

All Hodder Children's books are available at your local bookshop or newsagent, or can be ordered direct from the publisher. Just tick the titles you want and fill in the form below. Prices and availability subject to change without notice.

Hodder Children's Books, Cash Sales Department, Bookpoint, 39 Milton Park, Abingdon, OXON, OX14 4TD, UK. If you have a credit card you may order by telephone – (01235) 831700.

Please enclose a cheque or postal order made payable to Bookpoint Ltd to the value of the cover price and allow the following for postage and packing:
UK & BFPO – £1.00 for the first book, 50p for the second book, and 30p for each additional book ordered up to a maximum charge of £3.00.
OVERSEAS & EIRE – £2.00 for the first book, £1.00 for the second book, and 50p for each additional book.

Name ....

Address ....

....

....

If you would prefer to pay by credit card, please complete:
Please debit my Visa/Access/Diner's Card/American Express (delete as applicable) card no:

Signature ....

Expiry Date ....